GOING TO PLAYSCHOOL

For Rosie and the children
at Elms Road.

GOING TO PLAYSCHOOL

Sarah Garland

PUFFIN BOOKS

This is playschool

and here's your peg.

Time for a game,

then pouring sand,

rolling out pastry,

painting pictures,

dressing up and

undressing.

A rest and a drink of juice,

and outside to play.

Look at the rabbit!

A story before we go home.

Coats on, boots on,

but where's the rabbit?

Here it is! Let's go!